5/24

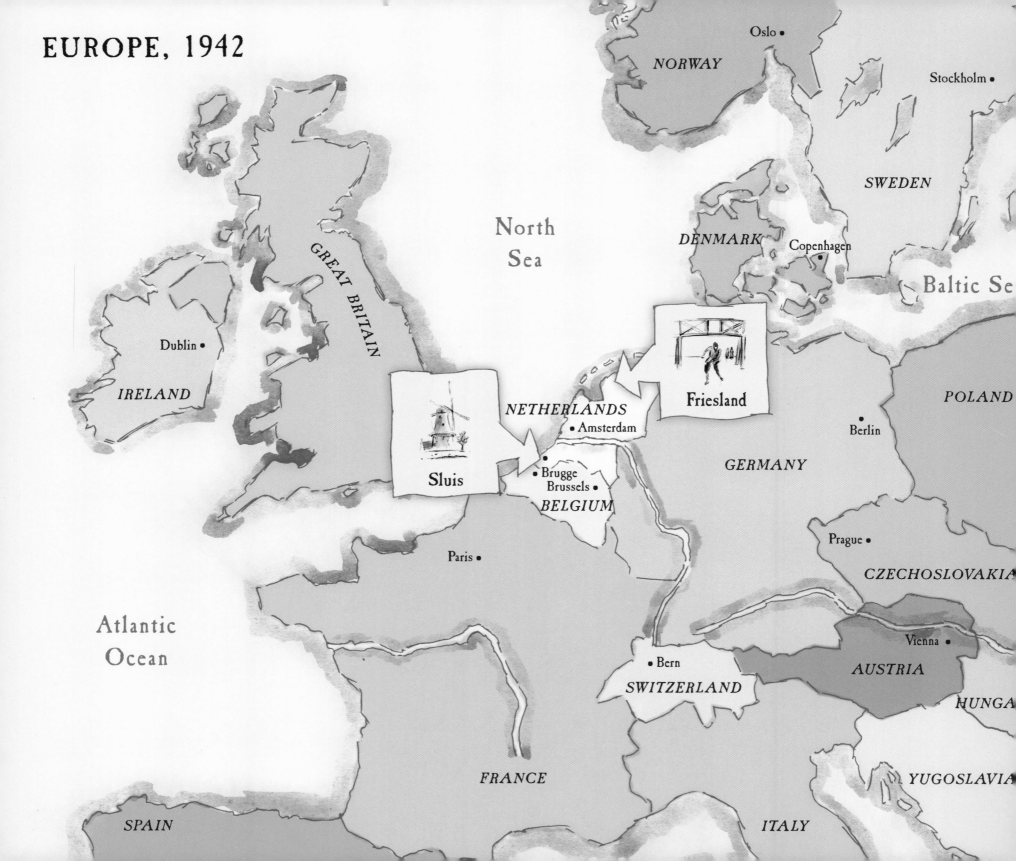

# EUROPE, 1942

Atlantic
Ocean

IRELAND

Dublin •

GREAT BRITAIN

North
Sea

NORWAY

Oslo •

Stockholm •

SWEDEN

DENMARK

Copenhagen •

Baltic Se

NETHERLANDS

Friesland

• Amsterdam

Sluis

• Brugge
Brussels •

BELGIUM

GERMANY

Berlin •

POLAND

Paris •

Prague •

CZECHOSLOVAKIA

• Bern

SWITZERLAND

Vienna •

AUSTRIA

HUNGA

FRANCE

YUGOSLAVIA

SPAIN

ITALY

# THE GREATEST SKATING RACE

*A World War II Story from the Netherlands*

## SKATING RACE

*For Margaret McElderry, with love—L. B.*

*For Margaret McElderry, my Great American—love, N. D.*

The author would like to thank the following people for their encouragement, stories, authentic details, and generous research assistance:

Belgium, Brugge, Damme, and the canal to Sluis: Martine Depreter and her family, Ivy Steinberger and Boekhandel De Reyghere, Jeannine and her mother (BVBA Gift-Shop), M. G. Keirsebilck-Croes (bridges), Cat Bowman Smith (winter canal and maps), and Marleen Agten.

Netherlands, the Elfstedentocht, skate manufacturing, and Sluis: Cees G. A. Janssen, Dita Ter Horst and the Netherlands Board of Tourism (NYC), Jelmer Kuipers (Fries Museum/Sneek), Walter Zandstra, Jacob De Jong, Carol Winkelman, Ernst Niewenhuis (Fries Skating Museum/Hindeloopen), the National Dutch Skating Organization, Cindy and Alex Curchin, Trish Marx, and June Sims.

Skating: John Dimon (Lake Placid, NY), who sharpened my speed skates for a few Olympic Oval laps, and Northland Ice Center in Cincinnati.

Special thanks to wonderful Polly Kanevsky and Niki Daly; to my husband, Pete; to M.K.M., who understood the vision for this book; and to our Leland friends Nancy and David Hunter who welcomed me to Brugge in September 1993 and showed me the canals by bicycle.

Margaret K. McElderry Books • An imprint of Simon & Schuster Children's Publishing Division • 1230 Avenue of the Americas, New York, New York 10020 • Text copyright © 2004 by Louise Borden Illustrations copyright © 2004 by Niki Daly • All rights reserved, including the right of reproduction in whole or in part in any form. • Book design by Polly Kanevsky • The text for this book is set in Caslon Antique. The illustrations are rendered in colored pencil, ballpoint pen, and watercolor with digital tone enhancement. • Manufactured in China • 2 4 6 8 10 9 7 5 3 1 • Library of Congress Cataloging-in-Publication Data: Borden, Louise. The greatest skating race : a WWII Story from the Netherlands / Louise Borden ; illustrated by Niki Daly. • p. cm. • Summary: During World War II in the Netherlands, a ten-year-old boy's dream of skating in a famous race allows him to help two children escape to Belgium by ice skating past German soldiers and other enemies. • ISBN 0-689-87440-5 • 1. World War, 1939-1945—Netherlands—Juvenile fiction. [1. World War, 1939-1945—Netherlands—Fiction. 2. Escapes—Fiction. 3. Ice skating—Fiction. 4. Netherlands—History—German occupation, 1940-1945—Fiction.] I. Daly, Niki, ill. II. Title. • PZ7.B64827 Gt 2004 • [Fic]—dc21 • 2002012040

FIRST EDITION

# THE GREATEST SKATING RACE

A World War II Story from the Netherlands

LOUISE BORDEN · ILLUSTRATED BY NIKI DALY

15439

Margaret K. McElderry Books

NEW YORK · LONDON · TORONTO · SYDNEY

In December of 1941 I was ten years old . . .
and at that time what I cared about most
was skating on the frozen canals of Sluis,*
the town where we lived.

I had learned this love from my father and mother.
In the Netherlands children learn to skate
as soon as they learn to walk.

My father was a skate maker by trade,
just like my grandfather and his father before that.
The tools in his workshop
had been handed down from father to son.
To many the Janssen name meant fine Dutch skates.
On the wall of our workshop was an old map of Sluis
and the canals that led to other towns nearby.

8    *Sluis is pronounced as SLOICE (as in "voice").

9

Even though Sluis is in the very south of the Netherlands,
we knew about the famous skating race:
the Elfstedentocht,* the Eleven Towns Race,
which is held in Friesland,
in the north of our country.

This race is held only in those winters that are very cold . . .
cold enough to freeze the canals and waterways
that connect eleven towns in this Dutch province.

Because I loved skating so much,
my hero was Pim Mulier.
Pim Mulier was a sportswriter,
and his name was known all over our country
because he was a very brave and strong skater.

On a December day, many years before I was born,
Pim Mulier skated to each of the eleven towns in Friesland.
And he skated this arduous route alone and in one day:
200 kilometers** along frozen canals and ditches
and across lakes . . . in bitter winds and in freezing temperatures.

*Elfstedentocht (Eleven Towns Race) is pronounced as ELF-STAY-DEN-TOCKT.
**1 mile is 1.61 kilometers. So 200 kilometers is approximately 125 miles.

Other Dutchmen had also skated from town to town.
But Pim Mulier's route,
in the coldest winter of that century,
became the first, the first *real* Elfstedentocht.

To prove to everyone that he had skated
to these eleven old and historic towns,
Pim carried a small red notebook with him.
In each town he knocked on the door of a house
and asked a citizen to sign his or her name
as well as the time of day.

Pim Mulier's time was 12 hours and 55 minutes,
a very, very difficult feat.

This is how our Elfstedentocht came to be
the greatest skating race in the world . . .
and why I wanted to grow up to be like Pim Mulier:
a strong, brave skater
who could skate 200 kilometers in one day
against a cold winter wind.

December of 1941 was in the second winter
of World War II in Holland.
For more than a year
our country had been held by German soldiers.
Life was the same in some ways,
and in many other ways it was not.
The soldiers were here in Sluis.
They were also in nearby towns
like Damme* and Brugge,**
across the Belgian border.

Because of the war,
my father was somewhere in England,
serving with the Allied armies.
My grandfather, Jan Janssen, had no workers to help him,
and there was little business.
The shelves of new skates were more empty than full.
Now my grandfather mended broken skates and sleighs.
He repaired worn-out shoes and boots
and saved every scrap of leather.

Many of our best skate blades had been seized
and shipped to Germany for the war effort.

"This is what it means to be Dutch,"
my mother told my sister, Nel, and me
on nights when the sound of German boots
on the cobblestones rang in our ears.
"Not only to love skating on our canals
but also to be brave in our hearts."

That Christmas
there were few gifts for anyone.
Yet somehow
my mother had found a box of paints for Nel
and a small red leather notebook for me . . .
the same one that now rests
on the shelf in our skate workshop.

*Damme is pronounced as DAH-MA.
**Brugge, also spelled Bruges, is pronounced as BREW-GHA; Bruges is pronounced as BROOJE.

For the next few weeks
I carried the notebook with me everywhere.
I wrote in it,
and I listed the names of each of the eleven towns in the race,
towns where I had never been.

I asked questions
and read about these towns in the books in my school.
I learned what was special about each town,
and then I wrote these things down in the leather notebook.
I even drew a map of Friesland
and marked the towns and the kilometers
on the Elfstedentocht tour.

I knew the name of each town by heart,
just as Pim Mulier must have known them:
first Leeuwarden, the capital of the province
and the starting point of his great tour . . .
then Sneek* . . .
then IJlst** . . .
then Sloten . . .
and Stavoren . . .
and Hindeloopen . . .
and then Workum . . .
Bolsward . . .
Harlingen . . .
Franeker . . .
and finally Dokkum.

*Sneek is pronounced as SNAKE.
**IJlst is pronounced as EELST.

Maybe someday, I, too,
would skate along the canals of these faraway towns.
Maybe someday, I, too,
would skate in the famous Elfstedentocht in Friesland.

I would learn what I needed to know.
I would train by skating long distances.
And when I was old enough to qualify for the race,
I would be ready to skate in this historic and national event.

That winter, and in the three hard winters that followed,
my grandfather and mother often helped others who were in trouble—
those who needed food or money or the trust of a friend.
Many people in Sluis knew that
the Janssen family was brave in this way.

There was a girl in my school,
one year younger than me.
Her name was Johanna Winkelman.
Of all the girls in her class,
Johanna was the best skater.
She could cut letters and words in the ice of the canal
with the blade of her skate,
like the long-ago Dutch poets.
My father had sold her family
several pairs of skates over the years.
The Winkelmans were good customers.
And they were fine neighbors to all.

One cold night in late January,
German soldiers came
and arrested Johanna's father,
a very brave man.
The Germans had learned
that he owned a hidden radio
and had sent messages to England.

This, of course, was forbidden.

The rest of his family was very afraid.
Mrs. Winkelman decided to send Johanna and her brother, Joop,
to their Belgian aunt, who lived in Brugge.
Maybe there the Winkelman children would be safer.
At least for the winter.
But how to get a Dutch girl and boy to Brugge
without any German soldier taking notice?

And there wasn't much time to make a plan.
The danger of staying was greater than the danger of going.

The day after Mr. Winkelman's arrest was a Friday,
and I remember every detail of that afternoon.
On Fridays my teacher always gave our class spelling tests.
Fifteen words a week.
That Friday I had written each spelling word right,
and I couldn't wait to tell my family
since spelling was a very hard subject for me.
I skated home from school with Nel, along the frozen canal,
waving that spelling paper in my hand.

I untied my skates and hurried into the workshop,
but my grandfather brushed my school paper aside.
Right away
I knew that something was wrong.

He put his hands on my shoulders and looked into my eyes.

"You're a strong skater, Piet,*
and you have a quick mind.
This is why I know you'll succeed in this important task.
I wouldn't ask you to do this if I didn't know it could be done."

My grandfather continued:
"Today you must be the best skater that you can be.
You must be as brave as your father . . . wherever he is.
You must be as brave as Pim Mulier!
You must skate the main canal to Brugge,
straight as an arrow to its mark.
And you will need to race against today's sun
to get there before dark.
I want you to skate as fast as you can,
but you must look like an unimportant schoolboy.
You will take Johanna and Joop Winkelman
and help them find their Aunt Ingrid's house.
We think this is the safest way to escape from those
who may wish these friends of ours harm."

Even though our country was occupied by the Germans,
skating was not forbidden.
There were few cars but many bicycles,
and when the waterways were frozen, many skates.
Still, where there were soldiers,
there could be questions.
And we would be skating across the border into Belgium,
our neighbor country.

*Piet is pronounced as PETE.

My mother sent Nel upstairs with her paint box.
Then she joined us at the workshop table.
Together we studied the faded map
that my grandfather had taken down from the wall.

"You will skate from Sluis to Damme
and then on to Brugge," my grandfather said.
He traced the route with his finger.
"You'll have to skate sixteen kilometers.
And you'll have to *klunen** at the bridges . . .
climb out of the canal and walk across on land,
and then climb back into the canal . . .
first near Hoeke,** then where two canals join,
and then at Damme.
Here and here and here."

My mother held out a bowl
of thick pea soup for me to eat.
"You must be careful," she said.

"There will be soldiers near those bridges."

My grandfather pointed to the maze of canals in Brugge.
I'd been to this beautiful town only by bicycle.
I'd never paid attention to the many canals.

"Listen carefully, Piet. When you get to Brugge,
you must skate here, under two bridges.
Then you will follow a row of linden trees.
They have been cut like fans.
Take the second canal to the right, then look to the left.
Ingrid Depreter's house is number nineteen, next to a bookshop.
It faces the canal and has a dark blue door.
She will be waiting."

My mother placed my warmest wool mittens and cap
next to my bowl of soup.
I saw a worry in her face that I had never seen before.

*Klunen is a Flemish word meaning "to walk on land in skates."
**Hoeke is pronounced as HEW-KA.

"If I can get an A on my spelling test,
then I can do this," I told her.

For the first time that afternoon
my mother smiled.
"Wim DeJong, who owns the bookshop,
is an old friend of ours, someone we can trust.
You're to spend the night at Ingrid's,
and in the morning
Wim will skate back with you to Sluis.
He has some books to deliver
to a Dutch customer."

That Friday afternoon, before I tied on my skates,
I folded my spelling paper into a small, neat square
and placed it carefully inside my Elfstedentocht notebook.
Then I slid the notebook deep into the pocket of my jacket.

I did this for good luck because I was very afraid.
I was afraid of the soldiers stopping us.
I was afraid that I wouldn't find the right canal
or the blue door of number nineteen.
And most of all, I was afraid of what would happen
to Johanna and Joop if I failed.

My mother saw me put the notebook in my pocket.
"Today, Piet, you will be a good guide.
I have faith that you will help Johanna and Joop find their way."

Quickly, my grandfather and I left.
We had no words, only hurry in our steps.
We clambered down to the docks, past the town boats
locked fast in the frozen canal.
How long would it take to skate those kilometers?
Joop Winkelman was only seven.
Would his legs be strong enough?
I was afraid to ask my grandfather,
afraid to add to his worry.

And then we were on the canal,
on the gray January ice dusted with snow . . .
pushing off, bending forward, finding our balance and our rhythm,
gliding, gliding, our chins tucked down against the wind.

I followed my Grandfather Jan's easy stride
and was proud that I could stay in his shadow.
He was tall, as many Dutchmen are,
and my grandfather *belonged* to that winter canal.

He was a part of it . . .
with every smooth step, his hands clasped behind his back,
always gliding ahead of me,
*swisssshh, swisssshh,* striding, striding, *swisssshh, swisssshh,*
the frozen canal gleaming like a pale Christmas ribbon
beneath his long-bladed skates.

Johanna and Joop were waiting for us
with their mother at the main canal.
They wore warm caps and thick wool jackets like mine.
Their schoolbags, lumpy with a few belongings,
were slung over their shoulders.

I took Joop's hand.
"You must pretend that I am your older brother today,"
I said with a smile.
I nodded to Johanna.
"And yours, too."

I could tell it was hard for Joop
to leave his mother's hug.
I put my hands in my pockets, feeling the notebook,
and looked away.
The war had brought hard things to Sluis.

We waved good-bye to my grandfather and Mrs. Winkelman,
and then we were alone, the three of us,
skating down the canal toward Damme . . .
four kilometers to our first bridge.

The ice was hard and smooth,
a dull winter mirror in the afternoon light.
The silent rooftops seemed higher as we glided past.

*Swissshh, swisssshhh.*
I could hear the scrape of our blades against the ice.
And I could feel the cold air inside my chest.
My legs were strong,
and I knew that Johanna could keep up.

But I remembered Joop behind us,
so I kept a slower, steady pace as I led the way.
"A great day for skating," I called in a loud schoolboy's voice.
Johanna took Joop's hand,
and we began to hum an old Dutch tune.

*Swisssshh, swissshhh,*
we swept over that ice in our skates
with smooth metal blades.

I turned to Joop:
"I think we should have our sister
spell a word in the ice after we *klunen* over the first bridge."
Joop nodded with bright eyes and a smile.

*Swiissshh, swisssh . . .* those Janssen skates gave me courage:
They had been made by my father.
The blue-gray sky was high and wide,
above the straight thin line of trees that bordered the canal.

We left Sluis behind and soon saw two German sentries
keeping warm in a guardhouse near the canal bank.
Here we would cross the border into Belgium.

"Keep skating and don't slow down,"
I whispered to Johanna and Joop.

I called to the sentries in Dutch and held up my red notebook
and spelling paper as we glided by on the gray ice.
"We're going to visit my aunt in Brugge . . .
and show her my schoolwork . . .
one hundred percent on my spelling!"

The taller sentry came out of the guardhouse
and called out a stern warning in German.
Then he fired a shot from his rifle above our heads.

The three of us turned and scraped to a sudden stop on the ice.
I held up my red notebook again.
Joop took my other hand and squeezed it hard through my mitten.
I squeezed his hand in return.
"Stay on the canal, Joop, with Johanna,
and smile your best smile," I whispered.

I scrambled up the canal bank,
slipping on my long skates.
The second guard grabbed my collar
and gave me a hard look from head to toe.
"Where are you going on that canal, boy,
on this cold afternoon?
State your name and business . . . *now*."
The guard spoke poorly in Dutch
and had a heavy German accent.

Before I could answer, he seized my red notebook
and turned the pages slowly, one by one.

"My name is Piet Janssen, sir.
My family are skate makers.
I am headed to Brugge with my sister and brother
to see our aunt.
She needs our help in gathering wood for her stove,
and I will repair her bicycle while I am there."

The German suddenly frowned
and stopped turning the notebook pages
when he saw the map I had drawn of Friesland's eleven towns.

"How interesting for a border guard
to find a book with a *map*, yah?

"Perhaps I will come to the conclusion
that you are a young *spy*, yah?
I find it strange that a bicycle mender
would be carrying a notebook with such a map."

He slowly tapped the notebook
against the palm of his gloved hand
and then handed it to the guard who held the rifle.

I dug the blades of my skates into the uneven ground
and remembered my mother's words:
"This is what it means to be Dutch."
I knew that I must show no fear.
And that I must be brave in my heart.

For a long moment the only sound on that canal
was a brittle broken branch skittering across the ice.
No words. Not in German. Not in Dutch.
I didn't turn around to look at Johanna and Joop,
but I could feel their cold fear against my back,
as indeed I could feel my own,
and the stern silence of soldiers who now held our country.

"The notebook is for school, not for spying.
*School*," I repeated carefully and slowly.
"I must write a report for my teacher on skating!"
I pointed to my skates.
"*Skating*. The great race of our country—the Elfstedentocht!
The map is of the eleven towns in a province up north.
A race for speed. A race for those who are brave and strong."

I pointed again to my skates.
Then I held out the spelling paper.
"And my spelling . . . to show my aunt in Brugge.
One hundred percent!"
I smiled a wide schoolboy's smile.
*Thump . . . thump . . . thump . . .*
My heart beat with an echo in the stillness of the canal bank.

Then the raw winter wind gusted across the low land
like a familiar Dutch friend.

"Elf-ste-den-tocht . . . ," the German spoke slowly,
and then nodded.
"Yah . . . the big race. I have heard of this race."
He lowered his rifle and nodded again.

In this cold winter
the race in Friesland was going to be held
in spite of the German occupation.
Even our country's enemy admired the sport
of speed on skates.
The tall guard pulled up his collar
and stamped his boots against the cold.

Then he waved me curtly with a gloved hand
back to the frozen canal:
"Your aunt in Brugge—she will be waiting
for her bicycle mender."

We had made it!
We could cross the border!

We had three bridges still ahead of us:
one at Hoeke and one where the canals joined.
Then the last at Damme.

All were too low to pass under on skates.
Skaters had to *klunen* at these bridges.
But if you were small and quick,
you could crawl under like a crab.
That's what we did.

At Hoeke
Johanna skated along one side of the canal
and Joop and I along the other.
We saw ice fishermen
and then some farm children on the canal bank,
but they only waved at us, so to *klunen* was safe.
There was no one here to fear.

At the bridge we stopped to rest,
and Johanna scraped *Pim* in the ice:
her first spelling word from her new big brother.
And then we were out on the canal again.
*Swiiissshh, swissshhh . . .*

I could tell that Joop's legs were getting tired:
He slipped and fell a few times.
But Johanna's were still strong.
She was a steady skater.
We were warm and cold at the same time . . .
warm from skating,
but the wind stung our eyes and our cheeks.

I gave Joop another promise:
"At the Damme bridge we'll rest again,
and we'll eat the sugar and sausage your mother packed for us."
*Swiisshhh, swiisssh . . .*
a few more kilometers were behind us.

The second bridge was as easy as the first.
Here the big canal that led to the sea crossed our canal to Brugge.
We saw a few people on the bridge road,
and a woman passed us on skates.
Out of the canal, *klunen,* and then back down on the ice.
I called out a second spelling word to Johanna:
"Try writing *Mulier.*"
Then I looked at the sun. It was lower in the sky.
"Just carve the *M . . .*"

As we skated on,
I told Johanna and Joop about the great Pim Mulier
and the very first Elfstedentocht.

I told them about each of the eleven towns
in Friesland,
far north of Sluis.
It was a winter afternoon, and we were skating . . .
for a while we almost forgot about the war.

But at the Damme bridge Johanna grabbed my arm
and pointed to four soldiers in a field nearby.
They were changing the tire on a truck.
We listened for their words: German!
Quickly, I took Joop's hand
and showed him how to slip under the low bridge,
like a crab.

We squeezed together in a huddle
and waited for the soldiers to drive away.
I held Joop's hand
and Joop held Johanna's.

The minutes moved by slowly.
One by one by one.
We waited. And waited.
Our toes and hands became numb.
But I didn't want those soldiers to see us, to ask questions.

I could feel the red notebook, wedged deep in my pocket.
I thought of Pim Mulier,
skating 200 kilometers through snow
and the fierce winter winds.
We needed only to skate 16 kilometers,
and we were more than halfway there.
Now I didn't feel as cold and afraid.

We heard the truck engine finally roar,
and the soldiers drove north toward the sea.
Brugge was south.
We pulled ourselves under the bridge
using our mittened hands and our elbows.
Then we were off again, flying down the canal.
In the dim distance I could see a smudge in the sky:
the tall tower at Brugge.

"Just five more kilometers!" I called over my shoulder.
Joop slipped and fell again, but he held back his tears.
My little brother was worn out.
We stopped and ate the sugar and sausages,
and I found a long, thin stick on the bank.
From then on, we skated one behind the other.

Johanna and I held the stick between us,
and together we pulled Joop along the canal.

We passed more skaters and a windmill,
then a big solid farmhouse with an ancient red roof.
We were very cold now from the wind—
too cold and too tired to hum a tune
or to talk or to notice the canal's row of tall poplar trees,
their trunks twisted by years of wind.
The schoolbag on my back was as heavy as a sack of books.

And then we were gliding through the Damse Poort,
one of the gates to the beautiful town of Brugge.

We had made it!
All those long kilometers were behind us.

Right . . .
hadn't Grandfather Jan said to go right?
But the canal joined with two smaller ones.
And my grandfather had said two bridges.
But which bridges?

I called to Johanna:
"Can you remember? Is it this way?"
She shook her head slowly.
"Everything looks different with the winter colors. . . ."

We stopped to catch our breath.
People were skating by, but I was afraid to ask the way.
There were Germans here.
I was afraid that I would ask the wrong question to the wrong person,
afraid of my Dutch accent in this big Belgian town.
Joop's lips were blue with the cold.
He hung on to the stick with wobbly legs.

I tried hard to remember all my grandfather's words.
The sun was almost down, and the winter air
seeped under my jacket and through my mittens.
Then I shrugged off the cold.
I was the oldest.
Johanna and Joop were counting on me.

"Let's go this way," I said firmly,
and we turned and followed the canal.
There, just ahead, was a stone bridge, ancient and gray.
We glided under the bridge
and heard the echo of our skates
in the dusk of this old, historic town.
Under another bridge that echoed again.
Then I saw the linden trees . . . cut like fans.
A group of skaters swept past, hurrying home before dark.

"Here!" I called to Johanna.
"We go here . . . to the right . . . the second right."

I saw the soft gleam of lights in the windows above us.
*Where* was the bookshop?
And where was number nineteen?
There were many doors on this street . . .
dark blue . . . and red . . . and brown . . . and green.
I could hear the clatter of bicycles on the street above.

The edge of the canal was rimmed with snow.

*Swisshhh, swisshhh . . .*
The ice wasn't smooth here in Brugge.
The lines of many skates crisscrossed the canal.
Johanna caught a blade in one of the ruts and fell.

As I turned to give her a hand,
I saw a sign for a bookshop
high on the row of houses above us.
Johanna dusted the snow off her jacket,
and we scrambled up the steps from the canal
to the cobblestone street.
I grabbed Joop and swung him around.
"Number nineteen, my little brother! See it?"

And there was the blue door,
and there was his Aunt Ingrid, waiting for us . . .
just as my grandfather had promised.

That night
I asked Johanna and Joop, and Ingrid Depreter,
to sign their names in my red notebook
and mark the time we had arrived:
*Brugge 5:16 P.M. 23 January 1942.*

The next morning
I skated home down the long canal to Sluis
with Mr. De Jong and his sledge of books.
As we waved good-bye,
I called out a last spelling word
to Johanna Winkelman and told her,
"Try tracing *that* one in the ice!":

## Elfstedentocht

# After the War

When the Allied forces freed Sluis in 1944,
my father returned home safely to our family.
After the war he continued making fine Dutch skates
with the help of my grandfather.

Mrs. Winkelman joined Johanna and Joop in Brugge
and lived with her sister, Ingrid, until the end of the occupation.
Johanna's brave father was sent to a labor camp in Germany.
He didn't survive the war.

Years later,
I *did* skate in my country's famous Elfstedentocht.
Twice I went to Friesland, far north of Sluis,
and skated to each of the eleven towns.
I did this in the cold winters of 1954 and 1956.
In 1954 my time was 12 hours.
In 1956 my time was slower due to fierce winds and snow.

I still have the red leather notebook that I carried to Brugge
the winter when I was ten.
It rests on a shelf in the old Janssen workshop.
And above it hangs my Grandfather Jan's faded map.
The pages of that notebook are thin but enduring.
There is the list of Friesland's eleven towns,
written in a boy's handwriting . . .
and Ingrid Depreter's signature next to Johanna's and Joop's.
Many in Sluis say that *this*
was my greatest race.

# THE ELFSTEDENTOCHT

*On 20 December 1890, Willem Johan Herman Mulier (1865–1954), a Dutch sports journalist, skated to each of the eleven towns of Friesland, a province in the northern Netherlands. Others had skated the same route, but "Pim" Mulier's was the first tour that was officially recognized. Mulier carried a small red notebook with him and had someone in each town sign his or her name and note the time. Pim Mulier skated this route of 200 kilometers in 12 hours and 55 minutes.*

*Mulier later helped organize an official Elfstedentocht race, which is held only in winters when the ice along the eleven-towns route is thick enough to skate on safely. Many consider this to be the most difficult skating race in the world because of its length and the severe winter conditions.*

*The first organized Elfstedentocht was held in 1909; other races that followed were held in the years 1912, 1917, 1929, 1933, 1940, 1941, 1942, 1947, 1954, 1956, 1963, 1985, 1986, and 1997.*

*In the most recent race almost seventeen thousand skaters participated. Usually three hundred of the participants are serious speed skaters. Many are unable to finish the race. Others skate the route but do not complete it in one day. This is an exciting, national event in the Netherlands. Businesses close, TVs are turned on, and classes are suspended in schools so that the entire country can enjoy the festive day and celebrate skating.*

*De Kroonprins heeft*
*Zwane Scaatsen*
*Koninginneschaats*

# The History of Skating

Families in the Netherlands and northern Belgium (known as Flanders) have had a tradition of skating on the canals and lakes of their regions for over four hundred years. Early European skates were crude, made from the shank bones of horses and cows. Skates were first used as a means of transportation over frozen waterways during cold weather. Roads were impassable. Farmers needed to get to village markets. Families needed to get to church. Skaters could travel long distances very quickly. Speed on skates was novel and exciting, and local races were held for men, women, and children. Several times during long-ago wars Dutch soldiers were able to defeat their enemies in winter by surprise attacks with a new weapon: skates.

Over the centuries iron and steel blades led to improved skates. Skating quickly developed into a winter sport and town celebration. Seventeenth-century masterpieces by Dutch and Flemish artists, as well as later paintings, depict games, races, and festivities on the local canals and lakes.

Early skates were also used in other areas of northern Europe. It is believed that Dutch and Flemish merchant sailors introduced skating to England. Later, British soldiers would carry this winter tradition to colonial America. And, of course, Dutch settlers brought their knowledge of skates to New York and the Hudson River Valley.

Today in the twenty-first century skaters all over the world find universal joy in this wonderful and ancient sport.